PANDAS' EARTHQUAKE ESCAPE

BY PHYLLIS J. PERRY
ILLUSTRATED BY SUSAN DETWILER

Liling and Tengfei, two giant pandas, woke with a start! "Tengfei" means soaring high, and there was nothing this cub loved better than sleeping where he was, high in a tree. But today something strange was happening. The tree in which they were napping had begun to sway. The two puzzled pandas clung tightly. The gentle swinging motion gave way to a whipping back and forth as the ground trembled beneath them. An earthquake!

As the shaking continued, the tree limb broke and fell. Liling and Tengfei came tumbling down. Surprised and frightened, Liling, the big mother panda, immediately checked on her cub. They had both landed on the ground among the leaves and branches but were not hurt.

The earth shook again. The wall around the nature enclosure where they lived came crashing down just a few feet from them. The two frightened pandas ran off. Liling led the way.

As they ran, the pandas could hear noise behind them— rocks knocking down trees, walls falling down, and people shouting. The two frightened pandas kept running.

Liling ran down a winding, two-lane road. Tengfei had grown quickly, but he was still a young cub who always stayed close to his mother. He followed right behind her now. Sometimes, in his fright, he made a squealing noise much like a baby lamb.

Liling suddenly left the road and turned into the woods.

Little Tengfei didn't see his mother ahead of him on the roadway. In a panic, he stopped, squealed, and looked around. Where was she? Where had she gone? Tengfei was all alone, lost, and didn't know what was happening. What was shaking his world?

Tengfei was frantic as he looked around. He stared deep into the woods. Suddenly he spotted the familiar black and white markings of his mother's fur. With a little cry of relief, he chased after her.

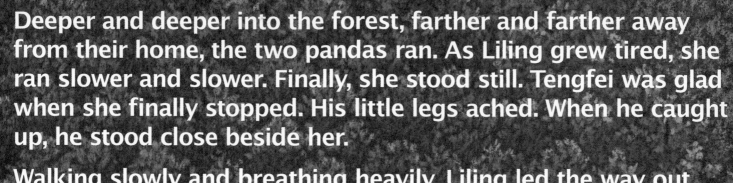

Deeper and deeper into the forest, farther and farther away from their home, the two pandas ran. As Liling grew tired, she ran slower and slower. Finally, she stood still. Tengfei was glad when she finally stopped. His little legs ached. When he caught up, he stood close beside her.

Walking slowly and breathing heavily, Liling led the way out of the trees and to the edge of a small valley. The stand of bamboo that once grew here had bloomed and died out.

Tengfei stared at this beautiful place. Bright purple and pink blossoms spilled across the ground. Tengfei thought he would like to play here.

Suddenly the earth began to move again. Liling found a safe spot for herself and Tengfei in a shallow cave in the side of a huge rock. Fallen tree limbs lay across the cave opening. The two giant pandas huddled close to each other in their secret, safe spot for hours until darkness fell.

Tengfei was hungry when he woke the next morning. He looked around. Where was his breakfast? Liling was hungry too, and she was thirsty. She led the way through the woods to a mountain stream. Liling and Tengfei took long drinks.

Liling poked at a plant bulb near the bank of the stream. She bent and ate it. It was tasty, so she ate another and another.

Tengfei watched. He had never seen anything like this before. These were not bamboo shoots, but he was really hungry. Finally he tried one of the bulbs. It wasn't so bad. He ate several more. While they were eating, the earth beneath their feet began moving again.

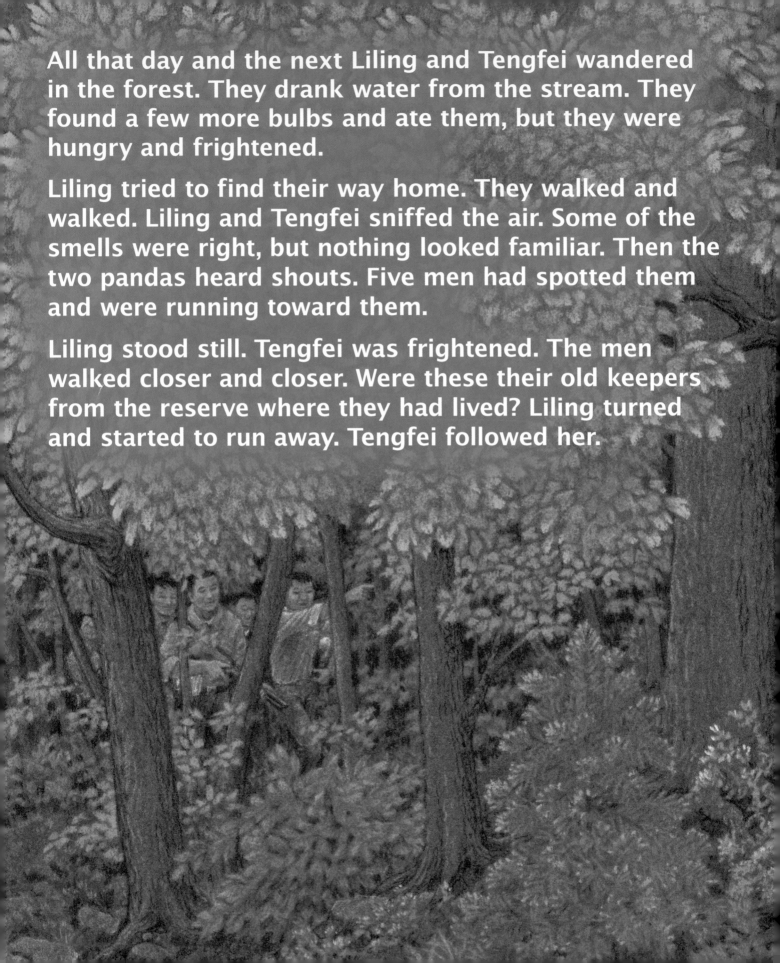

All that day and the next Liling and Tengfei wandered in the forest. They drank water from the stream. They found a few more bulbs and ate them, but they were hungry and frightened.

Liling tried to find their way home. They walked and walked. Liling and Tengfei sniffed the air. Some of the smells were right, but nothing looked familiar. Then the two pandas heard shouts. Five men had spotted them and were running toward them.

Liling stood still. Tengfei was frightened. The men walked closer and closer. Were these their old keepers from the reserve where they had lived? Liling turned and started to run away. Tengfei followed her.

Tengfei felt a prick in his shoulder and Liling felt a sting in her back. Both pandas slowed and dropped to the ground. One of the keepers who had been out looking for them had shot each of them with a dart. The darts had medicine to put both giant pandas to sleep.

The men carried the sleeping pandas from the edge of the forest back to what was left of their old home. They put them in a temporary holding pen they had built.

When Liling and Tengfei woke up, they were together at their old reserve. The men brought them armloads of bamboo shoots. The hungry pandas were really happy to be home. They sat and stuffed themselves for hours. Liling and Tengfei had survived the days the earth shook.

For Creative Minds

Endangered Giant Pandas

Giant pandas (*Ailuropoda melanoleuca*) are endangered. That means they are in danger of disappearing forever from the Earth (extinct).

They used to live in lowland areas that were cleared for farming. As the human population grew, giant pandas' habitats grew smaller and smaller. Now, wild giant pandas only live in cool, wet, cloudy high mountain forests in China—where bamboo grows.

Bamboo plants have mass die offs at the end of their life cycle, every 30-80 years depending on the species. In the past, the pandas could move to another area for more bamboo. Today, the pandas can't get from one bamboo area to another because of habitat loss and fragmentation—their habitat has been cut into sections and they can't get from one area to another.

There are 32 panda reserves in China, like the Wolong Reserve that was destroyed in the earthquake. These reserves provide a safe place for the giant pandas to live and get food.

It is illegal for people to hunt giant pandas.

Some zoos around the world have and breed giant pandas. These zoos work with the Chinese government to help protect pandas and their habitats.

Life Cycle Sequencing Activity

Put the giant panda life-cycle events in order to spell the scrambled word.

A	Cubs drink milk from their mothers until they are eight or nine months old and eat their first bamboo at about six months old. Cubs play, run, tumble, and climb
G	The female giant panda is pregnant for about five months and gives birth to one or two cubs in the summer—but usually only one survives in the wild. If born on a reserve, workers take the second panda to a nursery where they raise it.
I	Giant panda cubs are pink with short, white fur when they are born. They only weigh about 4 oz. (113.4 grams), and are about as big as a stick of butter. The black hair grows in when the cubs are about a month old.
N	Giant panda cubs stay with their mothers until they are about two years old. Then they leave to be out on their own. They are old enough to have babies when they are between five and seven years old.
T	Male pandas (boars) may grow up to 6 feet (1.8 m) and can weigh up to 250 lbs. (113 kg) while females (sows) usually weigh less than 220 lbs. (100 kg). Giant pandas live 18-20 years in the wild and 25-30 years in zoos and reserves.

Answer: Giant

When Liling and Tengfei woke up, they were together at their old reserve. The men brought them armloads of bamboo shoots. The hungry pandas were really happy to be home. They sat and stuffed themselves for hours. Liling and Tengfei had survived the days the earth shook.

For Creative Minds

Endangered Giant Pandas

Giant pandas (*Ailuropoda melanoleuca*) are endangered. That means they are in danger of disappearing forever from the Earth (extinct).

They used to live in lowland areas that were cleared for farming. As the human population grew, giant pandas' habitats grew smaller and smaller. Now, wild giant pandas only live in cool, wet, cloudy high mountain forests in China—where bamboo grows.

Bamboo plants have mass die offs at the end of their life cycle, every 30-80 years depending on the species. In the past, the pandas could move to another area for more bamboo. Today, the pandas can't get from one bamboo area to another because of habitat loss and fragmentation—their habitat has been cut into sections and they can't get from one area to another.

There are 32 panda reserves in China, like the Wolong Reserve that was destroyed in the earthquake. These reserves provide a safe place for the giant pandas to live and get food.

It is illegal for people to hunt giant pandas.

Some zoos around the world have and breed giant pandas. These zoos work with the Chinese government to help protect pandas and their habitats.

Life Cycle Sequencing Activity

Put the giant panda life-cycle events in order to spell the scrambled word.

A	Cubs drink milk from their mothers until they are eight or nine months old and eat their first bamboo at about six months old. Cubs play, run, tumble, and climb
G	The female giant panda is pregnant for about five months and gives birth to one or two cubs in the summer—but usually only one survives in the wild. If born on a reserve, workers take the second panda to a nursery where they raise it.
I	Giant panda cubs are pink with short, white fur when they are born. They only weigh about 4 oz. (113.4 grams), and are about as big as a stick of butter. The black hair grows in when the cubs are about a month old.
N	Giant panda cubs stay with their mothers until they are about two years old. Then they leave to be out on their own. They are old enough to have babies when they are between five and seven years old.
T	Male pandas (boars) may grow up to 6 feet (1.8 m) and can weigh up to 250 lbs. (113 kg) while females (sows) usually weigh less than 220 lbs. (100 kg). Giant pandas live 18-20 years in the wild and 25-30 years in zoos and reserves.

Answer: Giant

Giant Panda Fun Facts

Giant pandas have 11 different sounds they use to communicate with each other. Most adults communicate through scent markings, just like cats and dogs.

Pandas need to eat up to 40 pounds (18 kg) of bamboo a day! They also eat other grasses, flowers, or even small animals like birds or mice (omnivores).

Pandas get most of the water they need from the bamboo they eat.

Pandas spend 12 to 14 hours a day looking for and eating food, and the rest of the time resting.

Pandas' front paws have five digits with claws. Plus, they have an extra-long wrist bone they use like a thumb.

Giant pandas are white with black hair on their shoulders, legs, ears, eye spots, and muzzle. Scientists aren't sure why they are black and white, but think it may help them hide (camouflage) in the high mountain forests where they live.

Pandas have two layers of fur to keep them warm: a thick, coarse fur and short, waterproof underfur.

They can swim if they need to and climb trees (where they sometimes take naps).

Giant pandas walk on all four feet but sit upright while eating, like we might sit on the floor.

Shake, Rattle & Roll—Earthquakes

An earthquake can happen at any time—day or night. An earthquake might be too small to feel. But an earthquake can be big enough to shake things off shelves or even make buildings fall down—like the earthquake in this story.

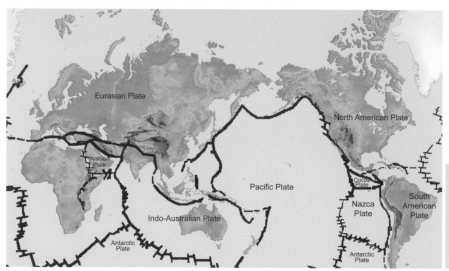

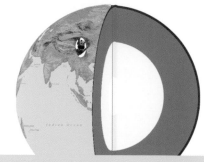

Crust: 5-25 miles (8-40 km)
Mantle: about 1,600 miles (2,600 km)
Outer core: about 1,400 miles (2,250 km)
Inner core: about 800 miles (1,300 km)

The Earth's crust is made up of "puzzle-like pieces"— called plate tectonics.

The Earth's crust puzzle pieces (plate tectonics) are always trying to push past each other but are jammed together and cannot move most of the time. The friction between them keeps them from moving sideways until a lot of stress builds up, and they finally move suddenly. If you compare earthquakes to snapping fingers, the plates moving past each other are like the fingers moving past each. The sound you hear when snapping fingers is from the air, but the sound of the earthquake is the ground vibrating.

Aftershocks are smaller earthquakes or vibrations that happen after the main quake. The aftershocks can be big too! They might happen right away, over a few days, or even years after the main earthquake. The bigger or stronger the main earthquake, the more aftershocks you will probably have and the longer you might feel them.

There are several different ways to measure the strength of an earthquake, but the most common one is the Richter Scale. It is not like the scale you have in your bathroom, but a number—usually between one and ten. The higher the number on the Richter Scale, the bigger the earthquake is and the more damage it may cause if buildings are nearby.

The vibrations travel away from the place the puzzle pieces (plates) pushed past each other (epicenter) in waves—just like waves you might make if you drop a rock into water. The vibrations will be strongest in the middle and seem to be less and less, the farther away from the fault they are.

The Richter Scale and Magnitude Ranges

0.0 to 0.9	1.0 to 1.9	2.0 to 2.9	3.0 to 3.9	4.0 to 4.9	5.0 to 5.9	6.0 to 6.9	7.0 to 7.9	8.0 to 8.9	9.0 to 10
Micro			Minor	Light	Moderate	Strong	Major	Great	
Not really felt by anyone.			Felt by a few people.	Felt by most people; dishes or windows may break.	Felt by most people, may move some furniture, some building damage.	A little damage to a lot depending on the type of building.	Lots of damage depending on type of building. Buildings may move off foundations, bridges may come down, objects may fly through air. Gas pipes may break causing fires.		

Where in the World?

On May 12, 2008, a major earthquake rocked parts of China. Measuring 7.9 on the Richter scale, this earthquake killed over 87,000 people and destroyed homes and buildings—including the Wolong Panda Reserve. Over 60 giant pandas were living at the reserve when the quake hit. The pandas have been moved to other reserves until the Wolong buildings are repaired and reopened.

Find the locations of the listed earthquakes on the map on the next page.
For older children: what are the grids or the approximate latitudes & longitudes for each of the earthquakes?

	Location	Date	Magnitude
1	Chile	May 22, 1960	9.5
2	Prince William Sound, AK USA	March 28, 1964	9.2
3	Sumatra-Andaman Islands	December 26, 2004	9.1
4	Kamchatka	November 4, 1952	9.0
5	Valparaiso, Chile	August 17, 1906	8.2
6	New Madrid Region, MO USA (series)	Dec. 11, 1811 to Feb. 7, 1812	7.2 to 8.0 estimated
7	Kanto (Kwanto), Japan	September 1, 1923	8.1
8	Michoacan, Mexico	September 19, 1985	8.0
9	Shensi, China	January 23, 1556	8.0 estimated
10	Eastern Sichuan, China	May 12, 2008	7.9
11	Chimbote, Peru	May 31, 1970	7.9
12	San Francisco, CA USA	April 18, 1906	7.8
13	Pakistan	October 8, 2005	7.6
14	Guatemala	February 4, 1976	7.5
15	Tangshan, China	July 27, 1976	7.5
16	Hebgen Lake, MT USA	August 18, 1959	7.3
17	Charleston, SC USA	September 1, 1886	7.3 estimated
18	Loma Prieta, CA USA	October 17, 1989	6.9
19	Nisqually, WA USA	February 28, 2001	6.8
20	Northridge, CA USA	January 17, 1994	6.7

To Annie Nagda, a friend and fellow writer, who visited the Wolong
Panda Reserve and first sparked my interest in the pandas, and to Casey
Miller and Yan Kung for helpful advice—PJP

To the victims, both human and animal, of the 2008 Sichuan earthquake—SD

Thanks to seismologist, Dr. Lucile Jones, Chief Scientist, Multi Hazards Project,
U. S. Geological Survey and author of *Earthquake ABC for Parents* for verifying
the accuracy of the earthquake information and to Elise Bernardoni, Education
Specialist at Friends of the National Zoo, for verifying the giant panda information.

Publisher's Cataloging-In-Publication Data

Perry, Phyllis Jean.
   Pandas' earthquake escape / by Phyllis J. Perry ; illustrated by Susan Detwiler.

   p. : chiefly col. ill., maps ; cm.

   Summary: A fictional story based on a real-life event, Pandas' earthquake
escape describes the adventures of a mother panda, LiLing, and her one-year
old cub, Tengfei, as they escape a panda reserve following an earthquake. Can
be used to teach children about earthquakes, animal survival, and a mother's
instinct to protect her child. Includes "For Creative Minds" section.
   Interest age level: 004-008.
   Interest grade level: P-3.
   Lexile Level: 580, Lexile Code: AD
   Also available in auto-flip, auto-read, 3D-page-curling, and selectable English
   and Spanish text and audio eBooks
   ISBN: 978-1-607180-715 (hardcover)
   ISBN: 978-1-607180-821 (pbk.)

1. Pandas--Juvenile fiction. 2. Earthquakes--Juvenile fiction. 3. Survival after
earthquakes--Juvenile fiction. 4. Pandas--Fiction. 5. Earthquakes--Fiction. 6.
Survival--Fiction. I. Detwiler, Susan. II. Title.

PZ10.3.P47 Pa 2010
[Fic]   2009937788

Manufactured in China, January, 2010
This product conforms to CPSIA 2008
First Printing

Sylvan Dell Publishing
976 Houston Northcutt Blvd., Suite 3
Mt. Pleasant, SC 29464